AND THEN CAME
HOPE

STEPHEN SAVAGE

NEAL PORTER BOOKS

HOLIDAY HOUSE / NEW YORK

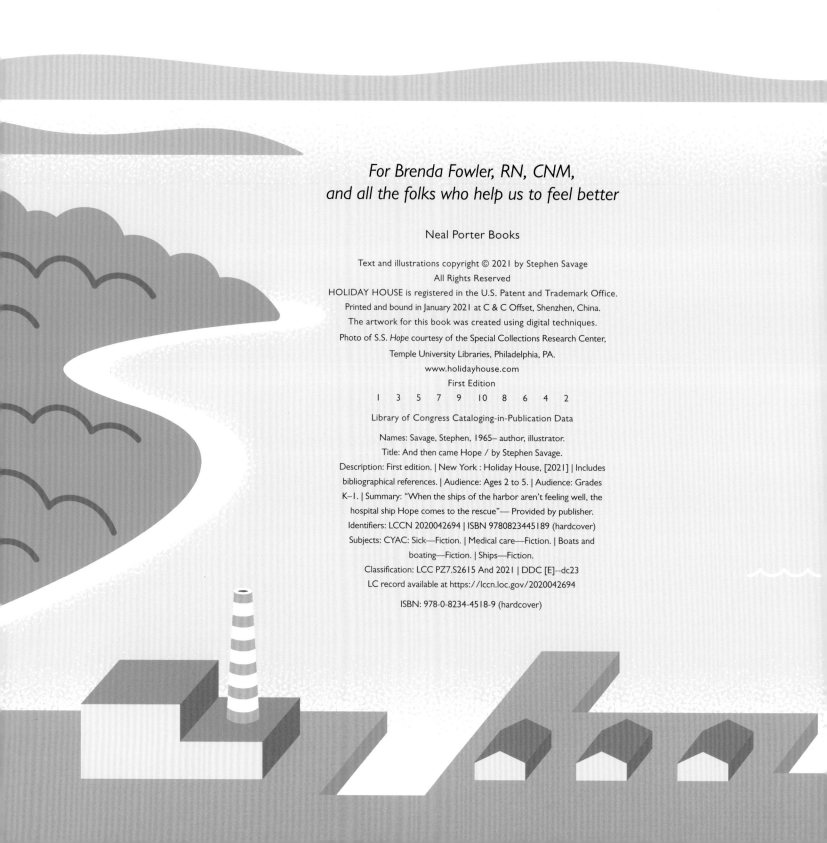

For Brenda Fowler, RN, CNM,
and all the folks who help us to feel better

Neal Porter Books

Text and illustrations copyright © 2021 by Stephen Savage
All Rights Reserved
HOLIDAY HOUSE is registered in the U.S. Patent and Trademark Office.
Printed and bound in January 2021 at C & C Offset, Shenzhen, China.
The artwork for this book was created using digital techniques.
Photo of S.S. *Hope* courtesy of the Special Collections Research Center,
Temple University Libraries, Philadelphia, PA.
www.holidayhouse.com
First Edition
1   3   5   7   9   10   8   6   4   2
Library of Congress Cataloging-in-Publication Data

Names: Savage, Stephen, 1965– author, illustrator.
Title: And then came Hope / by Stephen Savage.
Description: First edition. | New York : Holiday House, [2021] | Includes
bibliographical references. | Audience: Ages 2 to 5. | Audience: Grades
K–1. | Summary: "When the ships of the harbor aren't feeling well, the
hospital ship Hope comes to the rescue"— Provided by publisher.
Identifiers: LCCN 2020042694 | ISBN 9780823445189 (hardcover)
Subjects: CYAC: Sick—Fiction. | Medical care—Fiction. | Boats and
boating—Fiction. | Ships—Fiction.
Classification: LCC PZ7.S2615 And 2021 | DDC [E]--dc23
LC record available at https://lccn.loc.gov/2020042694

ISBN: 978-0-8234-4518-9 (hardcover)

The boats
in the harbor
weren't feeling well.

First Barge
got bonked.

Then Submarine
started shivering.

Ferry felt feverish.
She was steaming.

Aircraft Carrier
coughed.

And little Dory's nose was dripping.

She needed to see the doctor.

So they put
out the call.

And then came Hope . . .

dressed in white, with her team
of tugboats at her side.

Barge got
a big bandage.

Submarine snuggled up.

Ferry felt just fine.

Aircraft Carrier's cough calmed down.

All of the boats sailed away,
except for little Dory.

"You'll feel better soon."

Now the boats were shipshape.
But they knew if they ever
got sick again . . .

Hope would
always be there.

THE REAL S.S. *HOPE*

On September 22, 1960, a gleaming white ship left the San Francisco harbor and steamed across the Pacific Ocean to Indonesia. She would make eleven voyages over the next fourteen years, bringing medical care, training, and supplies to countries around the world.

The ship was the brainchild of Dr. William Walsh, who in 1958 persuaded President Dwight D. Eisenhower to donate a hospital ship called the U.S.S. *Consolation* to his humanitarian cause. The *Consolation* was refitted, updated, and given a fresh coat of white paint. Four giant letters were painted on her side: H-O-P-E. The letters stood for Health Opportunities for People Everywhere. And that's how the first peacetime hospital ship was born!

The S.S. *HOPE* was a state-of-the-art floating medical center with 250 beds, an operating room, an X-ray room, a library, and a pharmacy. The ship's most unique feature was a powdered milk machine called the "iron cow" that could make one thousand gallons of milk a day.

One hundred doctors, 150 nurses, and other allied health professionals, all volunteers, performed surgeries, vaccinations, treatment for injuries and trauma, and even dentistry. They shared their medical knowledge with the doctors and nurses in the countries they visited. The S.S. *HOPE* sailed on missions to Indonesia, Vietnam, Peru, Ecuador, Guinea, Jamaica, Nicaragua, Colombia, Ceylon (Sri Lanka), Tunisia, and Brazil (twice), always a welcome sight whenever she sailed into a harbor.

The S.S. *HOPE* completed her last voyage in 1974 and today she is retired. But her mission continues as Project HOPE, a land-based organization that provides medical care and training to countries hit hard by disease, war, and natural disasters. For more information visit Project HOPE at projecthope.org.